PUFFIN BOOKS

# Rita in
# Wonderworld

D1390715

# Rita in Wonderworld

### Written and illustrated by
## Hilda Offen

PUFFIN BOOKS

*For Billy*

PUFFIN BOOKS

Published by the Penguin Group
Penguin Books Ltd, 27 Wrights Lane, London W8 5TZ, England
Penguin Putnam Inc., 375 Hudson Street, New York, New York 10014, USA
Penguin Books Australia Ltd, Ringwood, Victoria, Australia
Penguin Books Canada Ltd, 10 Alcorn Avenue, Toronto, Ontario, Canada M4V 3B2
Penguin Books (NZ) Ltd, Private Bag 102902, NSMC, Auckland, New Zealand

Penguin Books Ltd, Registered Offices: Harmondsworth, Middlesex, England

First published 1999
1 3 5 7 9 10 8 6 4 2

Copyright © Hilda Offen, 1999
All rights reserved

The moral right of the author/illustrator has been asserted

Typeset in Bembo Schoolbook

Printed in Hong Kong by Midas Printing Limited

British Library Cataloguing in Publication Data
A CIP catalogue record for this book is available from the British Library

ISBN 0–140–38699–8

"Look! There it is! There's
Wonderworld!" cried Eddie.

"I can hardly wait!" said Jim. "I'm
going into the Ghost Grotto."

"Me too!" said Eddie. "I've heard it's
really scary."

"And I'm going on the Dino-Coaster,"
said Julie.

"What about you, Rita?" asked
Uncle Bill.

"Huh! Rita's too young for the
rides!" snorted Eddie. "She'd be
scared."

Wonderworld was packed.

"Phew! That was quite a drive!" said Uncle Bill, flopping down in the picnic area. "I need a nap."

"You can all go off on your own," said Auntie Sal. "But take care of Rita."

"Follow us, Rita!" said Julie. "We know just the place for you."

They stopped in front of a notice
which said "Chicks' Nest Play Area".

"Are you lost?" asked a lady in a
chicken outfit. She grasped Rita's hand.
"Come inside! I have a special little
tricycle you can play on."

Eddie, Julie and Jim ran away.

"We'll soon find your family," said
the Chicken Lady. "Now – what's
your name?"

Huh! thought Rita. I'm not going to
spend the day playing on a tricycle.

She jumped into the Ball Pool and
burrowed down till she was out of

sight. Then she took her Rescuer's outfit from her rucksack and started to change.

"My goodness! What was that?" gasped the Chicken Lady. It was Rita, shooting past her in a blaze of light!

"Now for some rescues," said Rita.
She didn't have to look far. Little
Kevin Tucker was crying his eyes out.
He couldn't steer his Bumper Bug and
everyone kept thudding into him.

Rita landed in the seat next to him.

"Hold tight!" she said and started to whizz Kevin round like a racing driver. They didn't hit a single Bug.

"Can we have another go?" asked Kevin as the ride came to an end.

But Rita was off again. She had heard a scream.

Victor the Viking had lost his balance! Rita caught him just before he hit the ground and set him back on his tightrope.

"It's best to try again as soon as possible," she said.

"I'll just practise quietly at the side," said Victor. "Can you show us how it should be done, Rescuer?"

So Rita rode Victor's unicycle
backwards and forwards across the
rope, juggled with six balls and
cooked a pancake – all at the same
time!

"Bravo!" cried the spectators. But
Rita was off. Her sharp ears had
caught the sound of a wail.

"I recognize that voice!" said Rita

Julie was standing by the Ghost
Grotto.

"Eddie and Jim went in!" she cried.
"But they haven't come out. Look –
their boat's empty!"

"I'll find them!" said Rita.

"But it's dark in there!" quavered
Julie. "It's full of ghosts and skeletons!
And bats and rats! And giant spiders!"
"They don't scare me," said Rita.
"Besides, I can see in the dark."

Inside the grotto, Eddie and Jim were caught in a huge spider's web. They were shaking like jellies.

"What ever happened to you?" asked Rita.

"We were trying to catch a bat," said Jim. "But we leaned too far."

Rita untangled them and flew them back to the exit.

"Hooray for the Rescuer!" cried Julie.

"I have to go!" said Rita. "I'm needed at the waterchute!"

Jenny Jones had shot from her spinning teacup! She whirled through the air and disappeared beneath the foam.

Rita did a running dive.

"Don't panic!" she said.

She held Jenny's head above water
and guided her down to the bottom of
the waterchute where her parents were
waiting.

"Make sure she does up her safety
belt next time," said Rita. "Uh-oh –
here we go again!"

There was trouble at the ticket
office!

"Stop, thief!" yelled Mr Wonder.

A gorilla had grabbed the takings
and was running off through the
crowd.

"Not so fast!" said Rita and she launched herself into a flying rugby tackle. The gorilla crashed to the ground.

"This is not a gorilla at all!" said
Rita. She whipped off a rubber mask.
"It's Larry Lightfingers, the well-known
bank robber!"

Mr Wonder came puffing up with a
policeman, but there was no time for
thank-yous. Something awful was
happening above their heads. The
Dino-Coaster was out of control and
travelling at the speed of light!

"Help!" screamed Julie. "I feel sick!"

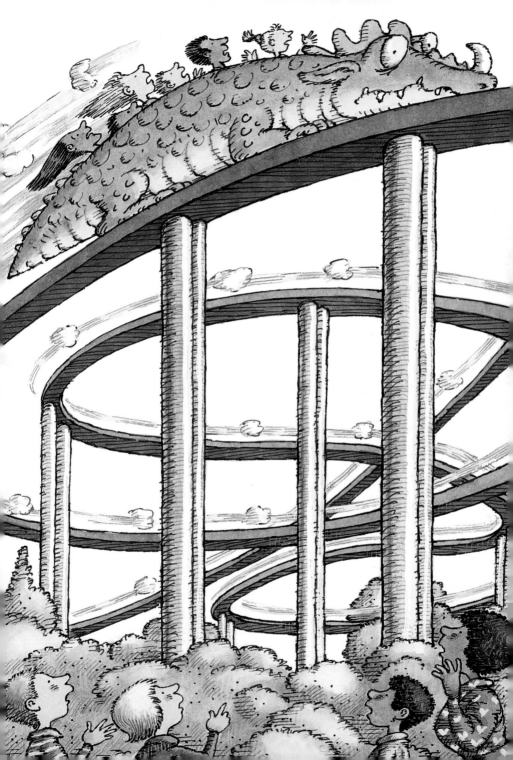

Rita zoomed upwards and caught
the Dino-Coaster by the tail. She hung
on as hard as she could and everything
ground to a halt.

"Three cheers
for the Rescuer!" cried
Mr Wonder as Rita pushed
the Dino-Coaster safely
back to the ground.

"You've just got to give me your autograph!" said Julie as she clambered down.

"Sorry!" said Rita. "Things to do!"

She could hear the lost children screaming in the Chicks' Nest.

"The loudspeaker's broken!" gasped the Chicken Lady.

"Leave it to me!" said Rita and she soared up into the sky.

"SILENCE!" she roared.

The Big Wheel stopped turning. The Pirate Ship stopped swinging.

Everything went quiet.

"WOULD ANYONE WHO HAS LOST A CHILD COME TO THE CHICKS' NEST – AT ONCE!" roared Rita.

Soon all the lost children had been claimed by their parents.

"Rescuer – please accept this Golden Ticket," said Mr Wonder. "It gives you free entry to Wonderworld for life."

"Oh, thank you!" said Rita. "Time I
was off, though."

She dived into the Ball Pool.

She had seen Eddie, Julie and Jim
coming to collect her.

In no time at all she had changed
back into little Rita Potter.

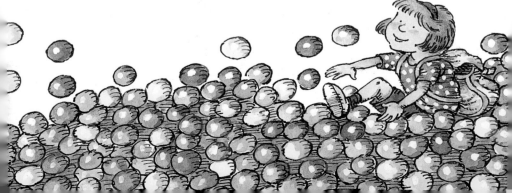

"So, Rita!" giggled Eddie on the way home. "How was the Chicks' Nest?"

"You missed the Rescuer again!" said Jim. "She got us out of the Ghost Grotto."

"And she saved me on the Dino-Coaster!" cried Julie. "She was brilliant!"

Rita smiled to herself and thought about her Golden Ticket.

"Oh well!" she said. "Better luck next time!"

*Also available in First Young Puffin*


## RITA THE RESCUER
### Hilda Offen

Rita Potter, the youngest of the Potter children, is a
very special person. When a mystery parcel arrives at
her house, Rita finds a Rescuer's outfit inside and races
off to perform some very daring rescues.

## ROLL UP! ROLL UP! IT'S RITA
### Hilda Offen

Rita is furious when she finds everyone has gone to the
fair without her. She's going to miss the fancy-dress
competition and a balloon ride. Then Rita remembers
her Rescuer's outfit. Soon she's ready to thrill the crowd
with some amazing stunts!

## SPACE DOG SHOCK
### Andrew and Paula Martyr

A talking space dog has crash-landed in Horatio's
garden! Horatio is delighted, but his parents can't wait
for their accident-prone visitor to go home. The trouble
is, Spog is stranded – isn't he?